date honey

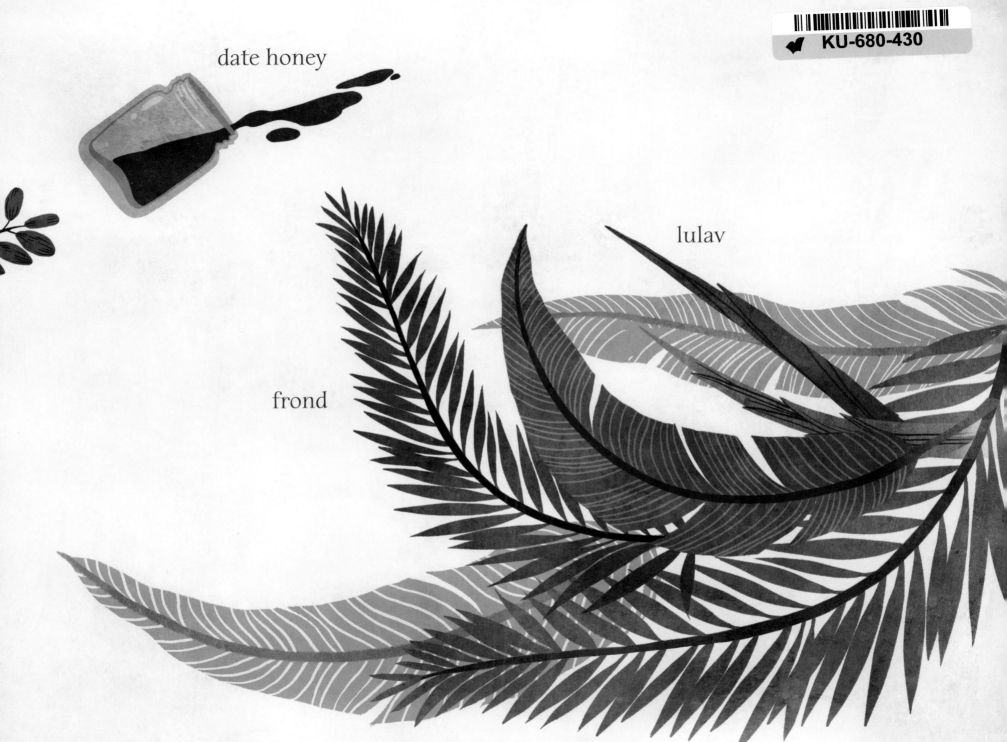

lulav

frond

Bare Tree and Little Wind

A STORY FOR HOLY WEEK

written by MITALI PERKINS

illustrated by KHOA LE

WATERBROOK

For Quiet Man

BARE TREE AND LITTLE WIND

All Scripture quotations are taken from the New American Standard Bible®, copyright © 1960, 1962, 1963, 1968, 1971, 1972, 1973, 1975, 1977, 1995 by the Lockman Foundation. Used by permission. (www.Lockman.org).

Text copyright © 2022 by Mitali Perkins
Illustrations copyright © 2022 by Khoa Le

Published in the United States by WaterBrook, an imprint of Random House, a division of Penguin Random House LLC.

WATERBROOK® and its deer colophon are registered trademarks of Penguin Random House LLC.

Library of Congress Cataloging-in-Publication Data
Names: Perkins, Mitali, author. | Le, Khoa, 1982– illustrator.
Title: Bare tree and Little wind : a story for Holy Week / by Mitali Perkins ; illustrated by Khoa Le.
Description: Colorado Springs : WaterBrook, [2022] | Audience: Ages 3–8
Identifiers: LCCN 2021001496 | ISBN 9780593234877 (hardcover) | ISBN 9780593234884 (ebook)
Subjects: LCSH: Easter–Juvenile literature. | Jesus Christ–Resurrection–Juvenile literature.
Classification: LCC BV55 .P425 2022 | DDC 232.96–dc23
LC record available at https://lccn.loc.gov/2021001496

Printed in China

waterbrookmultnomah.com

10 9 8 7 6 5 4 3 2 1

First Edition

Book and cover design by Sonia Persad and Annalisa Sheldahl
Cover illustrations by Khoa Le

SPECIAL SALES Most WaterBrook books are available at special quantity discounts when purchased in bulk by corporations, organizations, and special-interest groups. Custom imprinting or excerpting can also be done to fit special needs. For information, please email specialmarketscms@penguinrandomhouse.com.

He makes the winds His messengers.

—Psalm 104:4

The trees of the field will clap their hands.

—Isaiah 55:12

Little Wind skipped through Jerusalem's palm trees.

His visit made their green fronds clap.

Little Wind took a bow.

"One day we will clap on our own," Tall Tree said.

"When?" asked Little Wind.

"When Real King comes," Tall Tree answered.

Little Wind's next stop was Dead Garden.
Nothing grew there. Bare Tree stood
scarred with cuts and scrapes.
No fronds. No fruit. No flowers.

Little Wind tried to move her.
He puffed. "Where are your dates?"
She didn't stir. "Sold for honey."
He gusted. "Where are your seeds?"
She didn't budge. "Crushed for oil."
"And your fronds?" He was running out of breath.
"Used for a roof," she said.

Panting, Little Wind whirled around her one last time.
A few leftover shreds fell off her trunk.
"Thank you," Bare Tree said. "Those were itchy."
She'll never clap, Little Wind thought.
Not even if Real King comes.

Years passed. Little Wind visited Jerusalem again.
Tall Tree had big news.
"Real King is coming today!"
Little Wind whooshed through the grove.
The trees danced and sang.

Even Little Wind couldn't help getting excited.
He twisted up high for a better view.
Would he spot a noble horse? A crown with jewels?
A royal parade?

But all he saw was Quiet Man, still as a windless day.
Instead of a fast horse, a foal trudged along a dusty road.

People cut branches. They threw cloaks. Clapping and shouting,
they waved fronds for Quiet Man as if he were Real King.

In Dead Garden, Bare Tree was still bare.

No branches to stir.

No lulavs to sway.

No fronds to rustle.

But she was as joyful as the others.

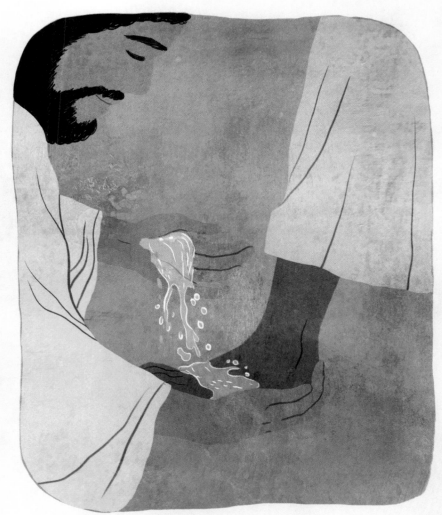

"Did Real King come?" she asked.

Little Wind wasn't sure. He told her about Quiet Man.

"Didn't look like Real King to me," he said.

"This was his first visit," Bare Tree said. "He will come back."

But then everything changed.
Quiet Man hung on a cross.
Little Wind cooled his face. Bigger winds came
to wail with sorrow. They ripped through the
curtain of the temple. Little Wind fled.

Strange news swirled around like a
breeze, and the winds began to whisper.
Quiet Man had been seen.
Here. And there. Alive. Not dead.
Could it be? Little Wind wasn't sure.
But he hoped so.

The next time Little Wind was sent to Jerusalem, soldiers galloped ahead of him. They drew swords and lit torches. "Burn every green thing!" a captain shouted.

The palm grove burned. Little Wind couldn't watch.
If he moved closer, he would spread the flames.

He swooped into Dead Garden.
Maybe he could keep them
from burning Bare Tree.
But a soldier with a
torch was at the gate.
Little Wind caught his breath.

The man jumped back on his horse.
"Nothing alive in there!" he called.
The soldiers rode on.

Little Wind rose high.
Everything in Jerusalem was gone.
Houses, gardens, markets.
Even the temple.
Bare Tree stood tall and stiff
against a smoky sky.
Embers glowed in heaps around her.
Little Wind didn't want to stir things up.
He blew away.

It was a long time before Little Wind
was sent to Jerusalem again.
He headed straight for Dead Garden.
There was Bare Tree.
Still scorched. Still lonely.

Little Wind swirled around her.
She didn't move.

But then he spotted something.
Was that . . . ? Yes, it was!
Bare Tree was sprouting golden flowers!
Little Wind danced around his friend.
"Wake up!" he said. She didn't answer.
Little Wind took a deep breath.
"WAKE UP!" he bellowed with all
his might.

Bare Tree stirred.
"What's happening?" she asked.
Little Wind told her about the crown of flowers.
"Soon branches will grow! And fronds! Lulavs too!"
He twirled with joy. Bare Tree's seeds
would fall to the ground.

A grove of her sturdy children would grow in Dead Garden.
Little Wind couldn't wait to visit them.

But Bare Tree had another plan.
"Take my seeds far and wide, Little Wind."
"Why not near and here?" he asked.
"Real King is returning," she said. "My children
must be ready to clap around the world."
So Little Wind got to work.

In fields, cities, meadows, plains, and villages, he scattered seeds.

Small trees started growing. Groves formed.

Little Wind told Bare Tree about each one.

She smiled. "Tell them to watch and wait.

Real King is coming soon."

Today some of Bare Tree's children are taller than Tall Tree used to be.
They give shade, dates, honey, and oil, just as their mother once did.
Little Wind travels everywhere to help them practice clapping.
He repeats Bare Tree's words on every visit.

"Real King is coming soon.
Watch and wait."
And they do.